Disney
M@ANA 2

We Are Voyagers!

By Erin Falligant

Illustrated by the Disney Storybook Art Team

A Random House PICTUREBACK® Book

Random House 🏠 New York

Copyright © 2024 Disney Enterprises, Inc. All rights reserved. Published in the United States by Random House Children's Books, a division of Penguin Random House LLC, 1745 Broadway, New York, NY 10019, and in Canada by Penguin Random House Canada Limited, Toronto, in conjunction with Disney Enterprises, Inc. Pictureback, Random House, and the Random House colophon are registered trademarks of Penguin Random House LLC.
rhcbooks.com
ISBN 978-0-7364-4505-4 (trade)
Printed in the United States of America
10 9 8 7 6 5 4 3 2

I am Moana of Motunui.

I am a *wayfinder*. With the wind in my hair and the sun on my face, I voyage across the ocean in search of new lands. It's who I'm meant to be! I've had lots of great adventures, which I share with my people whenever I sail home.

I like to teach others how to be voyagers, too.
Maybe I could teach you! Voyaging takes
some skills and a whole lot of courage. But if you're
called to the water like I am, you've got to
heed that call. So grab your oar and let's get sailing!
The **first thing** you have to do is . . .

...choose the right canoe!

I found my first canoe in the **Cave of Ancestors**. Gramma Tala led me to the hidden cave, which was filled with ancient canoes of all shapes and sizes. That was where I learned that I come from a **long line of voyagers**. My ancestors loved to sail on the open sea, too!

You'll want to choose a canoe with a **sturdy sail** and a **water-tight hull** (that's the body of the ship). Your canoe should also have a **cargo hold** big enough to store all your supplies—and maybe even a pet pig and a pet chicken, like my friends **Pua and Heihei**.

You'll need **a big canoe** because you'll want to . . .

...invite a whole crew!

You might think you can set sail with just a couple of friends, like the pig and the chicken I mentioned. Well, I'm here to tell you that pigs aren't all that brave. And chickens aren't all that smart (sorry, Heihei!). So you'll want to bring along a lot more friends than that.

First, look for someone who knows everything about canoes. My friend *Loto* can build them, fix them, and even sail them! She's always got *just the right tool* for the job, and she's not afraid to use it.

Next, you'll need a crewmate to record your adventures, like my friend Moni. He paints pictures to tell stories about the past and the present. Moni is also happy to control the oar when I'm busy doing something else. He sometimes forgets to steer because he's so busy painting, but hey, nobody's perfect.

You'll also want a crewmate who can harvest and grow food, just in case you're out at sea longer than you planned. I brought Kele the farmer on my last voyage. He can be grumpy, and it turns out he can't swim. Not. At. All. (Kind of wish he'd mentioned that before we set sail!) But give him a little dirt, and there's nothing he can't grow.

Who shouldn't you take on your voyage? Your baby sister, no matter how much she begs. She's not ready yet, but someday soon you can teach her how to voyage. Until then, just remind her that the ocean connects the two of you. So no matter where you go, you'll always be together.

Now that you've said your farewells, it's . . .

...all hands on deck!

Once you hit the water, it's **smooth sailing** ahead, right? Not exactly. You and your crew will need to work hard to learn a few voyaging skills.

Feel the ocean's current. Is it hot? Cold? Which way is it flowing? The current can tell you a lot. Just don't fall in!

Keep an eye on the **stars** overhead. They're like a **map in the sky**, guiding you in the right direction.

Adjust the sails to catch the wind. That's how you'll get to your destination faster!

You and your crew will need to **work together** to keep the canoe on course. And pretty soon all that work will start to feel fun. Nothing is better than voyaging!

But you'll probably experience a few **not-so-fun** things out on the open water, too. Like . . .

...running into enemies!

You might encounter, say, an **enormous ship** filled with **Kakamora**, little spear-carrying coconuts with a big attitude.

But don't judge others too quickly. Your rivals don't always want to fight you. And every once in a while, they can even become friends!

It probably won't happen right away. I mean, the Kakamora will likely hit you with their blow darts first, which turns your arms and legs into jelly . . . and, sure, the cure involves being slimed by a giant blobfish.

But you may discover that the Kakamora are just a little homesick. And if you work together, you can all get where you want to go.

And while you're keeping an open mind, don't forget to . . .

...let others guide you.

If you meet a not-so-friendly demigod on your journey, listen to what she has to say. Demigods have **thousands of years** of experience, so you can learn something from even the **battiest** of them.

Like when I met **Matangi**, a demigod living in a giant clam. I wasn't so sure about her and her creepy bats at first. But she taught me something important: **Don't be afraid to get a little lost.**

Voyagers don't always know where they're going. But that's the whole point, right? You're trying to find something that has never been found! Chances are that you'll have fun **discovering new paths**! But in your **scariest moments** at sea, you can always . . .

. . . count on your crew!

I mean, **things are gonna happen**. Things you don't expect. For example, say you fall into a portal and burst out of a **whirlpool** with your canoe spinning like crazy. To survive that, you'll have to **lean on your friends**.

My best friend also happens to be a demigod, which really comes in handy. **Maui** can use his magical hook to turn himself into a hawk, a shark, a lizard, and even a bug to **save the day**—or just to make me laugh. And in my darkest moments, Maui **believes in me** until I start believing in myself again.

Just know you can always . . .

...brave the storms together!

At sea, the weather can change in a heartbeat. When a **storm blows in**, your crew will definitely freak out. They'll ask to turn the canoe around or hide in the cargo hold. That's when you have to **step up** and **be strong**. Remind them that sometimes the only way past a storm is to **go straight through it**.

Ask your crew to help you with the sail and the oar. Give everyone a job to do to keep their minds off their fear. And if your demigod bestie offers to help you battle the storm? Let him! The surest way to survive a storm is to stand together.

When you reach new destinations—and you will—make sure to . . .

. . .celebrate!

Let others know you've arrived. How? Climb to the highest part of the island and blow into your conch shell. *Bawooo!* Isn't that the best sound? Call to all the people of the ocean, and then listen as the sound ripples across the water. . . .

Shh . . . Do you hear anything? If you're lucky, someone else will answer you by blowing into their conch, too! That's how you'll know there are *other people* nearby.

Voyagers from different lands are ready to greet you and tell you stories of their homelands. You can swap plants and seashells and other **treasures from home**. You can study their canoes and learn how to improve yours. I mean, we're all **people of the same ocean**, right? But **your job** as a voyager isn't done yet. Now it's time to . . .

...share what you found with those you love.

I love to bring tales and treasures home to my little sister, Simea. I want to share the whole ocean with her, just like Gramma Tala did with me.

After your big adventure, I hope you'll **keep voyaging**, like I did. The horizon is just the starting line. You have so much more of **yourself** to explore! I believe you will become a **great voyager**, someone your people look up to. And if you can go beyond the obstacles you encounter, you will **sail farther** than you ever imagined you could.

And if you **love voyaging** . . .

...teach others, just like I taught you!

Keep the **tradition** going. Follow the stars. Seek out new shores and islands. Chart new paths across the sea . . . because there's always more ocean to discover, more to share with those you love. After all—**what could be better than this?**